READING CORNER

Pedro the Pirate

Written by
Mick Gowar

Illustrated by
Rory Walker

W
FRANKLIN WATTS
LONDON•SYDNEY

Mick Gowar
"I'm not very brave, or big, or tough, so if I were a pirate I'd probably be a lot like Pete. I hope I'd have someone like Pedro to look after me!"

Rory Walker
"I always wanted to be a pirate and sail the oceans in search of adventure and hidden treasure!"

Pete was a pirate captain.

Most pirates are brave and fierce.

But Pete wasn't.

Pete's crew weren't brave or fierce either. They got scared when the cannons went bang.

They hid when the muskets went crack.

Pete had a parrot called Pedro.

Pedro *was* brave and fierce.

He was also very clever.

He could say: "Pretty Pedro!"

and "Pedro wants peanuts!"

Pedro listened carefully when the cannons went bang and the muskets went crack.

One morning, Pedro showed just
how clever he was:

"BANG! BANG! CRACK! CRACK!"

BANG!! BANG!! CRACK!! CRACK!!

"Help!" shouted the pirates. "We're being attacked! What shall we do?"

"To the lifeboats!" cried Pete.
They got in the lifeboats
and started to row.

Then they saw who was making all the noise. "Bother and blow, it's Pedro!" said Pete.

"What shall we do now?"

asked the pirates.

"Row back to the ship!" cried Pete.

17

That night on the ship, Pete and his
pirates were woken up by loud noises.

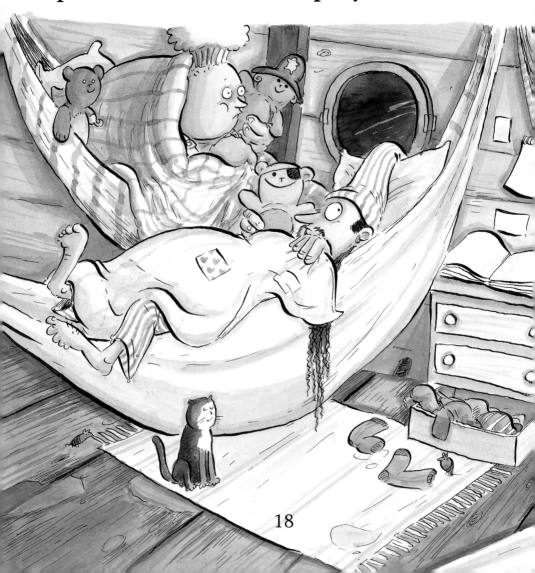

BANG! went the cannons.

CRACK! went the muskets.

"What shall we do?"
asked the pirates.

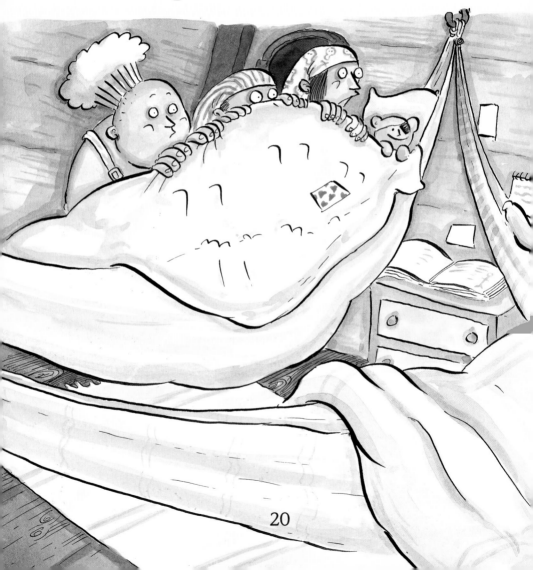

"Go back to sleep!" said Pete.

"It's only Pedro."

But it wasn't Pedro.
It was Bonecrusher Bill
and his fierce
pirate gang!

23

The fierce pirate gang jumped on to Pete's ship. "Tie their hands, then make them walk the plank!" cried Bonecrusher Bill.

Then Pedro had a good idea:

"BANG! BANG! CRACK! CRACK!"

"Help!" shouted the fierce pirate gang.

"We're being attacked!"

"Get back to our ship!"

shouted Bonecrusher Bill.

Pedro pecked the ropes.

Pete and his pirates were free!

"Three cheers for Pedro, our new pirate Captain!" shouted the crew.

31

Notes for parents and teachers

READING CORNER has been structured to provide maximum support for new readers. The stories may be used by adults for sharing with young children. Primarily, however, the stories are designed for newly independent readers, whether they are reading these books in bed at night, or in the reading corner at school or in the library.

Starting to read alone can be a daunting prospect. READING CORNER helps by providing visual support and repeating words and phrases, while making reading enjoyable. These books will develop confidence in the new reader, and encourage a love of reading that will last a lifetime!

If you are reading this book with a child, here are a few tips:

1. Make reading fun! Choose a time to read when you and the child are relaxed and have time to share the story.

2. Encourage children to reread the story, and to retell the story in their own words, using the illustrations to remind them what has happened.

3. Give praise! Remember that small mistakes need not always be corrected.

READING CORNER covers three grades of early reading ability, with three levels at each grade. Each level has a certain number of words per story, indicated by the number of bars on the spine of the book, to allow you to choose the right book for a young reader:

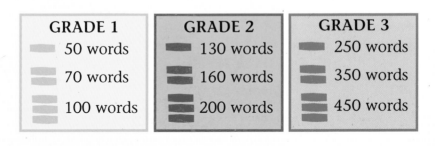

GRADE 1	GRADE 2	GRADE 3
50 words	130 words	250 words
70 words	160 words	350 words
100 words	200 words	450 words